The Choice

A NOVELLA

NIKALA ASANTE

Dedicated to those taking the great spiritual journey to make sense of it all.

CHAPTER 1

I could feel the wounds in the soles of my bare feet bleeding against the rocky ground, but I kept running. My shoes were still back at my sleeping space with my pack and my knife. If only I hadn't gone back to free others from this life of misery! But, I *had* to because I remembered...

I remembered so many lifetimes of being taken across the Atlantic and enslaved in the Americas. At times, I had poisoned the White men and burned their houses, murdering them and their families. Other times, I had slipped away quietly to survive in the forest alone. And of course, there were lives where I ended myself by jumping into the ocean.

Yet, this fierce loop of forced labor in the Americas continued. Each time that I thought death and rebirth would bring me a new situation, I was disappointed. I was stuck in this cycle of being born on the West coast of Africa repeatedly, living peacefully until my teen years approached, and then, being whisked away as a prisoner of war to be sold into captivity.

But long ago, before this loop began, I was truly powerful. So much more powerful than now. I was a healer and an oracle helping many with my gifts on both coasts of The Continent. I was a part of many groups over thousands of years, many cycles of death and rebirth. My skin has worn all shades. And, I remembered. I remembered all of it.

Retaining my memories across lifetimes was not a problem until this past 200 years. I suffered the trauma of recollecting every loss, every torture, and every heartbreak while others forgot it all each time they were reborn.

Considering the countless tragedies within this holocaust, their forgetting may have been a gift. However, most also forgot their ancient identities and divine power. They had been broken. Detached. Truly enslaved.

In this life, they called me a sorceress. I did not call myself that. How could I? Being connected with the many spirits that linger beyond most's perception was not sorcery. It was natural. Using plants and touch to heal; these were our God given gifts.

However, even the Blacks called me this name. Did I hold it against them? No. They didn't know better. If they did, they'd be sorcerers and sorceresses too.

It was not my mission to judge. My goal now was to free as many as possible. Too many times, I had witnessed them being brutalized, spiritually and physically. Yet, I abandoned them time and time again for my own solitude.

In the past, I blamed them instead of the circumstances that brought them to this. I looked down on those who didn't fight, didn't run, didn't try anything to make a change. Then, I met someone who changed me completely. I met someone who did resist, with both her being and her actions. She walked and talked like she knew freedom and didn't know slavery. Fannie.

Fannie was a beautiful young woman of maybe 30 years who looked as if she belonged in a palace, not on a plantation. Although her skin was like honey and her hair was wavy and long, she was made to work the fields because she had a "smart mouth". She respected herself. I admired her for that.

"I'm getting out of here," she told me one day.

It was soon after I was brought back to this hellhole called "The South" located in North America. This time, I was 17 years old. She said I had "wise eyes", not realizing I had been alive for many thousands of years and painfully recalled the lessons from each one.

"I will be happy to join you," I replied, smiling.

Her plan was to take some food and supplies from the house to sustain us. Apparently, I was not the only soul she told. Word had it, the White man of this place was waiting for her when she slipped through the kitchen window for the supplies.

They burned her alive as an example. We were forced to watch. As the tears littered my face, my heart burned not with anger, but for the first time in this strange land, with love.

I loved this woman, yes. Yet, and this is what surprised me most, I also loved those who held so much fear inside of them that they felt obligated to stop her from seeking freedom.

Did they feel they would be rewarded within bondage? There is no reward until the chains are broken. How many of these atrocities did you have to see, hear, feel, and smell before you lost all hope and willpower to be free?

This was... compassion. No longer did I want to run away from them; *I wanted to teach them why liberation was important, so they could run with me.*

And by the grace of the Great Creator, I succeeded. It was slow, so slow. Quiet conversations in the field, humbling myself to gather thorny cotton that scraped thin cuts into my hands when I knew I had the power to walk away silently at any time, burning the plantation to the ground.

I knew I couldn't teach them directly about freedom; I'd end up like Fannie. Although I didn't fear death, I did not strive towards physical pain either. Not without a purpose. So, I spoke to them in parables like the man in their Bible - Jesus. Parables and folktales from my many years in Africa.

They asked me how I knew so many stories; I made up a grandmother who was rich with culture. A grandmother I had been snatched from and whisked to America. Truly, I'd had a multitude of grandmothers and been a grandmother as well, more times than I could count.

They came to love me. Women competed to walk next to me through the crops. Men gathered in my cabin over cornbread and red beans to hear more tales.

As the years passed, their voices deepened and their backs straightened as the connection grew between their present selves and the roots they'd forgotten. It was almost time.

I had now lived about 40 years. While my skin and body was still youthful, I'd never married as I didn't feel this was a life for children. The White man forced me on several occasions to lie down for him or for men known to breed strong boys, but they didn't know the power of this "sorceress".

At any time, I could have killed them with ease, even from a mile away. But, I chose to suffer out of love. My job wasn't finished.

Yet, one thing I wouldn't do was bring a baby through me to suffer too. I chewed my herbs in secret to remain barren. There were too many children already suffering here and if I could free them, that would be more rewarding than giving birth to a hundred seed.

We planned, we prepared, and those who were ready left with me. We succeeded in reaching a free state called Ohio. It was a long and arduous journey, but so worth it to see the amazement and relief on their beautiful brown faces.

Once they were settled and on their way to gainful employment, I knew what I had to do. Though it was a suicide mission, I knew had to return for those left behind, those who didn't believe it was possible.

I had to tell them the stories of their friends and loved ones who were now free and then bring them with me to also enjoy new lives. Whatever happened, they would know a love like none other - the love willing to come back for them. Fannie opened my heart to this love with her determination to live a free life and her willingness to strive to bring others along.

Once I reached the plantation, everything seemed to go even better than expected. Men, women, and children gathered into a communal candle-lit cabin with me and we shared a magical night of stories, tears, food, smiles, hugs, and laughter with no interruptions.

Yet, the reality was, I was a fugitive. Hours later, my morning hiding place in the woods was raided by White men with dogs. Though I had not revealed my sleeping location to anyone, I noticed a scrap of my dress was missing. I suppose someone had sliced it away during the excitement to lead the dogs to me and to betray me as they had betrayed Fannie.

I would not return the betrayal by abandoning this opportunity to be the love. Instead of running deeper into the vast safety of the woods to hide myself, I ran *towards* the plantation. They all came out to watch as the barking dogs hailed my entrance.

"No matter what, I will come back for you!" I yelled as I sprinted. "If you can't find your own way to freedom, I will come back for you! I will always return!"

I was smiling. Many were crying but were too afraid to step forward and try to assist. Some turned or bowed their heads. I didn't know if they were praying or if they were ashamed.

As I approached the big house, I gathered a handful of hay from the ground and blew it, chanting three words. It burst into flames. I threw it through an open window, chanting the three words again. The flames grew and engulfed the kitchen. No more hiding my powers. They needed to know I was serious.

As I resumed sprinting, I heard obscenities being screamed by the White men. Some stopped to tame the fire. A few kept after me. I couldn't run forever. This was no life to live. Instead of using more magic, I relaxed into this moment and allowed myself to feel what those felt who had lost connection. Limited.

Using only my feet to carry me, I ran until my soles ached and bled, until the dogs caught up and tore my flesh apart. I stood imperceptibly next to my mutilated body, joyous that I did it all differently this time around.

And, I would keep my promise. I would come back for them. If only I'd known what that would involve.

CHAPTER 2

I was home. Not with the Yoruba or the Akan people, not even with the Nubians. I was in my true home with my family. Once again, I wore my white cloak and I was filled with an insurmountable peace.

"Welcome," my mother said, pulling down the hood of her blue cloak before embracing me. The smile across her deep cocoa face was as welcoming as her arms; it was as welcoming as the warm waves of the ocean after they had been bathed by the sun.

"I am so happy to be here! Is it over now? Can I stay here with you?"

I had not forgotten my promise to the people on the plantation, but the elation that quivered through my chest and pulled tears down my cheeks... how could I leave it to endure another bout of sorrow and tragedy?

"You know that is not possible. You have not completed your work," she replied.

"Ascension is a ways off, but not so long," Father said, embracing me next.

He wore a white cloak like me and his countenance was pure, gleaming white light with flecks of violet. He never bothered with a human form when he wasn't walking on Earth.

"What did you learn, daughter?" Mother said, still beaming exuberantly.

Wiping my tears, I spoke, smiling.

"I learned compassion! I truly desired to teach them all to reconnect with the Creator, even the ones who hurt others. Even the ones who hurt me."

"Nothing can ever truly hurt you," Father interrupted. "It's only a dream where souls go to evolve."

"It feels real! When I'm there, nothing is realer. This, you - you are the dream! Even with my memories, I feel so far away from you. Almost like I've never known you."

"We understand more than you know," he replied, hugging me again. The light emanated from him through me, dissipating the pain I'd brought with me.

"Yes, I know," I responded, re-aligning with my mission as I healed.

"You know you have to go back. But, this time will be different. This time you have a choice," Mother said.

"What kind of choice?" I asked.

"The time of Awakening is soon to come. You will go to the people who need you most, those who were in bondage for thousands of seasons. You will teach them all you've learned."

"I don't understand. How is that a choice?"

"As a thousand years is as a day in the eyes of the Great Creator, one life is as many thousands. Truly teaching one person is teaching the world. Your choice is in *who* you will teach."

"I've crossed paths with so many. How could I choose?"

"Who needs you the most?"

"The people I just left," I replied with quick certainty. "They were so broken."

"And of them? Which one needs healing the most?"

I closed my eyes and thought back on Fannie, the White man, the women who cooked and those who picked cotton, the men who served and those who toiled in the fields; still, I was at a loss as to who to choose. I just wanted to stay here. But, it was not my time to remain.

I thought harder... the betrayer! There was someone whose name I didn't know who had been inundated with a fear so intense, it had been my demise. Maybe Fannie's too.

"Who cut the scrap from my dress? Did you see?"

"Yes, we saw everything. We were always watching, always walking with you. You know that," Mother replied.

"That is who I think needs me the most," I answered.

Father's light brightened as it did when he was very glad.

"You are making a strong choice," he assured. "It will be the most difficult journey yet. But, after this, you can rejoin us forever."

"I'll do anything!" I exclaimed, more excited at the idea of being home for eternity than I was at the prospect of guiding this individual.

"Thank you, beloved. Would you allow me to show you something first?" Father requested.

"Of course."

With a wave of his palm of light, rays emitted, and a picture appeared before me. It was a brown boy, drawing in the dirt with a stick. He must have been about 7 years old; his eyes still glowed with the wonder of being alive.

As the images flashed forward, the boy grew older. At about 10, he wandered too far away from the property where it appeared he was kept against his will. After being brought back by men with dogs, he was taken into a shadowy shed where a gorgeous mahogany horse stood alone. At least, it seemed as if it had once been gorgeous. Now, its neck hung low, and it's mud-caked coat was bald in patches.

"See this horse?" a White man said. "You just like this horse - property. This horse try to run away, we gone bring it back. This horse break a leg, we gone kill it. We ain't got no use for horses can't work. Now, you been off in the clouds too much like you can't work neither. What you think we should do to you?"

"You gone kill me?" the boy asked with wide eyes. His eyelashes hailed the sky like flower petals. He was a beautiful boy. I could sense the light in him too. It was one of the strongest energies I'd ever sensed.

"Is he an angel?" I asked Father.

"He is divine, as all humans are," he answered. "But even the most divine must forget and relearn before Ascension. Now, please watch."

I re-focused on the story being presented.

"Kill you, you can't work. Naw, what I got in store for you ain't so easy. You need to know who you belong to."

The White man brought in three Black men with blank stares and bowed heads. They looked as if their souls had been taken from their bodies. A mist of shadows surrounded them; their auras had been stained thoroughly.

"Show this black piece of shit what happens when you don't know your place!"

The men gathered around the boy like vultures. He held his hands up protecting his face. Then, the unthinkable happened. They each took his small body like he was a woman as he screamed and cried. Their stoic faces were unattached to his agony.

The White man watched and laughed, smoking a short, fat piece of cigar. The gray smoke from the cigar mixed with the shadows around him. He was stained too, I saw now; even more densely than the three men.

The image shifted to the boy being a man, now wearing an empty stare and a cape of shadows. He was forced to do to other boys what the men had done to him and was just as unconcerned about their pain.

Then, I saw myself, as I had been in my most recent life. I was about 21 and being escorted by the same White man with a firm grip to my arm. I couldn't believe I didn't recognize him before. He was much older now and the landscape of the property was very different, but this was the same "Master" and plantation from the life I'd just left.

"Ain't got no use for no Black bitch won't make babies," he said, pulling me to the shed.

The boy, now a man with a hollow gaze, entered the shed soon after. He ripped my skirt and took me violently as the White man watched. I had never been with a man. It hurt and I bled, but I didn't cry. I wouldn't give them the pleasure.

I hadn't anticipated this. The boy who once drew happily in the dirt became the broken man who robbed me of my virginity.

"Why are you showing me this?" I asked Father, turning away.

"Please, keep watching," he instructed.

Although I felt anger rising within me, I turned back to the visual. The image shifted to show Fannie telling the man how she was going to leave and how she wanted him to come too, to be away from all this heartache and affliction.

"I know what happened to you," Fannie said.

"You don't know shit! Just shut up. Ain't no getting away from here. Ain't nobody ever got away," he replied with a twisted face.

"I got a plan. I'm gone get some food and supplies tonight from the big house and get out. Even got a map. You ain't got to be doing this no mo'. I know what he got you doing to the girls. And the boys..."

"Shut up, bitch! You don't know a damn thang!" he responded, slapping her forcefully.

"Alright, then. I'll leave it alone. It's just... I wanna see you with something better."

She walked away, melancholy wetting her eyes.

The image changed again, showing him behind me with a pocket-knife, slitting off a scrap of my skirt that pooled on the dirt floor as I squatted and told tales of freedom.

"He was responsible! For Fannie! For me!" I cried. "He... he hurt me with his body. Then, to send those men after us! She was burned alive! I was eaten! I don't know. I've changed my mind! I don't want to help him."

"You've already agreed," Father rebutted. "That's why I wanted you to see this, so you could understand how he became this way."

"No one has to be this way! He had a choice too. He could have chosen to call on God. He could have healed!"

"How could he call on God when he doesn't even know God?"

"Well, how could I ever help him? What could I say that he would understand? He didn't listen to Fannie!"

"You can't *talk* to him. He won't listen. He still hasn't healed. But, you can *show* him."

"Show him what? This?" I yelled, waving at the fading light projection.

"Show him love."

I was far from eager to encounter this damaged soul again, but I allowed the feeling of compassion to fill my heart again. Fannie was brave enough to try to save him. I would be brave too.

"What if I fail?" I asked.

"As long as you are demonstrating love, you cannot fail. Love changes everything, even when it doesn't seem that way," Father answered.

Mother was now looking away. I could feel her. She didn't want this, not really. She wanted me to be here with her. And, there was something else. Something she wasn't saying.

"What is it, Mother?" I inquired. She was silent.

"She's our *daughter*!" she exclaimed, facing Father.

"That's why this is so important. We've already discussed this, hundreds of times. She will survive. We will be with her, healing her constantly, bathing her in love and light."

"But will her light survive?" Mother asked him, frowning. This was the first time I'd ever seen her frown.

"Certainly! She is so strong, one of the most resilient warriors that has ever walked the earth! Do you remember when she stood up against the army in the East? Even the men ran, but she stood valiant without even a spear to do battle!"

"And, they captured her!" she countered.

"And, she revolted again! On the ship! But most importantly, after all this time, she has never lost her love and never lost her light. Even with her memories..."

"She can't keep them," Mother interrupted. "It would be too painful."

"Yes, you're right. She will have to forget. If she remembers us, she will try to leave her body again. She will try to come home. This is too important. She has to forget, and we must block the exit."

"What are you talking about?" I shouted. Never had I seen my parents like this before. Arguing like humans!

"I'm so sorry," Father said dully. His light faded greatly, until I could barely see him. "We can't let you take your memories this time. We will give you the gift we've given many, the gift of forgetting home."

"How is that a gift?" I wailed, tears resuming.

Home was the only reason I could bear to go back to earth again and again. I always knew it would end, that I would come back to them. Even when my faith was thin, in my heart, I felt home offering me an eventual reprieve.

"We are running out of time. The Awakening must happen soon; you will see it and be a part of it within this lifetime. We do not have the luxury of allowing you to end your life and return as a baby over and over like before."

"Like when I was being brought into slavery? What could be that hard? Anyway, won't I be on another plantation? Or will I be a child on the same one as before?"

"Slavery will have ended, at least in its overt physical form. Yet, mental slavery will be prevalent," he responded.

"Then what?" I thought about the worst case scenarios. What could frighten Mother so much? "Oh, I see. I know what this is. I will have to marry him, won't I? I will have to be the wife of the soulless man."

My tears were not stopping. I didn't feel like a strong warrior like they said. Right now, I felt like a little girl about to be separated from everyone who loved her and sent into God knows what.

"No," Mother answered, looking down as she continued. "I'm so sorry. You will be his daughter."

I couldn't even imagine! He would certainly slap me around, gazing with those vacant eyes. He would kill me!

"He won't kill you. He will love you," Father replied, reading my thoughts as he always did.

"Then, why do I need to teach him love?" I was so confused.

"Because the way he loves, it will not always feel like love. He does not know how love is supposed to work," Father explained. "Now, we are out of time. We must send you now."

I swallowed back my cries and braced myself for the fall. Mother and Father hugged me tight in a huddle and said in synchronicity, "We love so much. We will always be with you. Be strong. Be brave. One day, you will be ready to remember who you are."

With these words, I fell into the gaping expanse of earth's atmosphere as a beam of light, speeding more quickly than any human could discern. I could see other streams falling around me - hundreds, if not thousands. Suddenly, I was tangible. Darkness and water surrounded me, and I felt trapped.

Where was I? Who was I? My mind was blank. This was terrifying.

"Let me out!" I yelled, but no words came out of my mouth. Mouth, I knew this word. I knew many things, but I did not know who I was or why I had been locked away.

"Push!" I heard in a male voice. Then, a woman screamed. As if I was propelled by her scream, I emerged into the cold air, held by pale, forceful hands.

"Put me down!" I cried, but my words were not understood.

I looked around. The room was bright with whites and silvers, but the faces were dark. Not dark in color; the woman I had come from was brown and the man was a pinkish-white, but there was a dark shadow around them. An... aura. Yes, that's the word. They had an aura of sadness. The word I wanted was...

disappointment. No one was happy to be here. No one was happy to see me. I screamed again, this time not trying to speak, but letting my cries pierce the icy air. I knew I didn't want to be here, but what else was there? I had come from that wet darkness and I didn't want to go back. What else was there?

There was nothing; only this.

CHAPTER 3

I stared out the wide picture window of the unfinished house into the vast green field beside it. My grandmother's house was incomplete inside – wooden rafts separated certain rooms instead of walls and walls that did surround rooms were plain with white plaster, yet to be painted. However, every piece of furniture was in place for me to dance around in glee.

Breathe. I inhaled and exhaled. How did I know how to breathe? How to speak? I was alone, as I was often, yet I knew so much. It was amazing. It must have been the man in the sky that we prayed to - God. God must have taught me all that I knew.

Still breathing in and out in amazement, I walked through the living room, touching the maroon cloth couch, the large, dark wooden table, and then, through the long hallway, glancing at my small brown face in the giant, unframed mirror on the right-hand wall, to my great grandmother's room. I wasn't really alone. She was always there, usually sleeping. Climbing into her soft bed, I snuggled into her right arm. She startled awake.

"Hey, baby. What you doing?" she asked, wrapping her arm around me.

"Nothing," I replied, kissing her cheek. Love. That's what this was. "I love you sooo much!" I said, kissing her again.

"I love you too, baby," she replied, returning my kisses.

We didn't talk every day, but she often held me when I cried, and anytime I wanted, she let me brush her long, silky hair. One time, I asked her how she got hair like that. My hair was short and thick, hard to comb except with a hot pressing iron and blue grease. She told me she was part Indian - Blackfoot.

Sometimes, I would read the Bible to her. A day when she felt talkative, she told me she had never learned to read. I didn't understand; I was only five years old and I could read. She was in her eighties.

"Girls ain't learn nothing like that when I was growing up," she explained. "I picked cotton and took care 'a my lil' brothers and sisters. Cotton look soft, but it hurt. Make yo' hands bleed. Walked here from Mississippi when I was 16, barefoot. Ain't have no shoes til' I was grown."

She told me how she got married when she was 22 and then started having babies. She shared how she didn't love her husband and he didn't protect her. She had to carry guns to fight off White men who tried to hurt her and take her land.

"Got a gun right here, 'case somebody wanna be foolish and try something now," she said, touching a small gun in the bottom of her nightstand where she kept her brush.

"Ain't nobody gone hurt us, Mother."

"Never know what might happen."

And, no one did try to hurt us. Ever. We were so safe and I was so happy, even when the house was quiet and it felt like I was in the world by myself. I had older sisters, but they were nearly always out with their friends. Then, there was my grandmother, Mama Lena. It was her house we all lived in and she also ran a nightclub in front of the house. She was up there working day and night. My mama was there too, working behind the bar, serving drinks. When my mama was at home, she was quiet like a ghost. But, she wasn't home much since the club was so busy.

Every now and then, they would let me come in the club at night. With the reds, blues, and greens of the disco ball spinning above me, I would walk from table to table, playing cards with the grown folks and taking sips of their drinks out of red cups until I felt dizzy. The black plastic-topped tables folded out on four feet; so flimsy, you couldn't even stand on them.

If I had a quarter, I'd put it in the jukebox and play some of my favorite blues songs. I loved to dance and sing along. When it was daytime and I didn't want

29

to be in the house, I'd go out in our big yard and look for white flowers poking through the ground to pick and make bouquets. Mama Lena called them weeds and said we needed to cut the yard when they grew. I loved them and wish they could grow tall, never getting cut. I loved the grass when it was so high, I could almost get lost it in it. Grasshoppers would jump up on me as I laid there, talking in their language I couldn't understand. The sky was a perfect blue everyday. Everything was so perfect.

Nighttime could be scary when I was in the house with just Mother, though. It didn't just get dark, it got dark dark. Seemed like there was no light anywhere. Her room was a million miles away, down a hall filled with monsters. I knew about monsters from the movies I watched with my uncle Frank sometimes. They could only come out when it was all dark because they were scared of the light.

I stayed in my room, wishing I had a night light or that I was brave enough to risk turning on the room light and Mama Lena seeing it from the club out front. She would come home and grab her leather belt, telling me I was running up the electricity bill. Not wanting a whooping, I pulled the blanket over my head to shield me from the darkness. Only thing that made me feel better was when Mama Lena said I could come out to the club or when my daddy came and got me. He made me feel safe; I wasn't even scared of the whooping I would get for sneaking away. It was worth it.

I had to keep it secret and quiet when my daddy came because he was "doing bad", Mama Lena said. She pointed a gun at him one time and warned, "Don't come 'round here." But, I loved my daddy. He was so nice. He would knock on the window real soft so that if anybody was home, no one would hear but me. I heard him every time. When I opened the window, he would give me a peppermint and a big hug and kiss. I'd get some food from the kitchen, like chicken and biscuits or sandwiches, put on my jacket, and slip out the window to go with him.

No one told stories like him! He knew the Bible up and down. As he walked, I sat on his shoulders listening to tales of Daniel and Nebuchadnezzar. Sometimes, he told me real stories about how he had to steal because he hungry or how he had to fight my mama because she was "cheating on him".

"What that mean? Cheating on you? Like cheating in a game?" I asked.

"That mean she didn't love me. She loved other men," he explained.

"I don't love no other man. I just love you."

"You love your uncles."

"Not like you, Daddy. I love you most of all!"

"That's why you my baby. You the only one who love me. You the only one who never turned against me and won't never hurt me."

Then, he'd spin around with me still on his shoulders so I could feel like I was flying! I'd hold my arms out and he'd grab my shins to balance me so I could be like a real bird! Afterwards, we'd keep walking for what seemed like forever and then came to one house or another. When we got inside, he'd be with other men, holding pipes with orange fire. They weren't pipes like my Paw Paw used to smoke before he died; they looked different. I didn't like something about these places. There were shadows all around, more shadows than there were men. I'd sit against the wall with my arms around my knees and pretend I was a doll. Nothing could hurt a doll, and a doll wasn't trying to hurt anybody either. Then, everything would go black, blacker than a dark dark night alone at home.

"Daughter, we are with you," a voice said.

I was in a large room with no walls. Everything was white as far as I could see, except a bright light that shone with a hint of purple.

"Where am I?" I asked.

"Be brave. Be strong. I'm so sorry."

When I opened my eyes, I was back on Daddy's shoulders, walking home in the warm sunlight. He was quiet, sad.

"What's wrong, Daddy?"

"Ain't nothing wrong. You want some pecans?" he asked, pulling brown hulls full with sweet meat from his pocket.

"I love you, Daddy," I said, as I ate the pecan flesh he gave me after cracking it in his mouth.

"I love you too. More than anything in the world."

CHAPTER 4

After some time, I got older, as all girls do. Mother and Mama Lena passed away and Mama was still moving around like a ghost. When Mama did smile or hug me, it felt like everything was right in the world. Then, she'd get silent again like her voice brought her out of a hiding place she never wanted to leave. I was 15 now. Daddy was in jail for the third or fourth time. Possession of crack/cocaine again. We didn't talk often anymore. He'd stopped taking me out the window when I was 6 or 7, then he got kind of distant over the last couple of years, even when he wasn't in jail. I asked him why; he said he missed his boys. He had two boys by another woman; they both died as teenagers a few years back. Sickle cell and heart failure. They had never come around much, so I didn't miss them; I just felt sad that I had never gotten to know them. If I had known them, I could feel how he felt. I wanted to share his pain.

One of my older sisters had gone off to college and the other was out with her friends every day. I busied myself with school and reading books. When that got old, I started getting boyfriends. Boyfriends felt like brothers, but they wanted sex with me. Some lasted three weeks and some three months, but they all said the same thing like they'd rehearsed it together.

"Let me put the head in."

"Just taste it. Put your mouth on me."

"Just let me taste it."

"Let me stick my fingers in it."

"Come on, you ain't no virgin. Ain't nobody no virgin no mo'."

I'd heard it all. Eventually, I gave in, just to see what it was all about. My sister who wasn't in college had sex all the time; she even had a baby. It was a quiet baby who would sit with my quiet mama and just be quiet all the time. Having a penis inside of me wasn't all that, but I loved the feeling of arms around me, lips kissing my lips. It made me feel closer to something that felt missing in my life, something I couldn't name. This something - I wanted it so badly. I started drinking, getting high with the boys, taking pills that made me feel floaty and want sex, but I still couldn't reach that something. I got close though, every time.

One day, when I was 17, I met a man who was different from the boys I'd been letting inside me. He was almost 30. When he talked to me, he was really talking to me, not just trying to get in my panties. He told me about his life, how he was in and out of foster homes, beat up and cursed out by adults who didn't really want to be parents. After a few weeks, he asked me to move in with him. I was ecstatic! Somebody really loved me, really wanted to be around me. He bought me gifts every week - cards, teddy bears, pretty dresses. We kissed everywhere! Didn't matter if we were on the bus, at the grocery store, or walking down the street. He was the most affectionate person I'd ever met.

Then at times, he was mean. He would push me against the wall and ask me where I'd been all day. *I've been at work, you know that,* I'd reply. I'd quit school to waitress so I could pay the bills. He had a job too, but he spent his money on music equipment or to get some weed to help his creativity. It was important that I was supportive; he was the first man who ever really loved me besides my daddy. Daddy was still in jail, so I didn't see him at all. The prison he was locked up in was far away. He never wrote us with the address. I wasn't sure why; I missed him so much.

But Tev - my boyfriend - he reminded me so much of Daddy. He told long stories like Daddy used to tell. I'd stay up and listen all night, even if I had to be at work early. When he was mean, I'd forgive him like the Bible told me to. He was so sweet; how could I stay mad at him? Like Daddy, he'd say, "You're the only one who loves me. You're the only one who never leaves me. You're the only one who believes in me." And when we'd make love! It wasn't having sex, it was *making love.* Steam would rise from our bodies and

I'd feel the closest I'd ever felt to that "something" I'd been seeking. And it wasn't just all of that, he would listen to me too. He was interested in my life.

"What was it like for you growing up?" he asked me one day.

"It was good. I had my grandma, Lena, my great grandma, Fannie, my mama, my daddy, and my sisters, and sometimes, uncles, aunts and cousins would come around. Other times, it felt like there was no one in the house but me. But, I was happy."

"Fannie? That's a name I never heard before."

"Yeah, we called her Mother. She was a strong woman."

"You look pretty strong. You ever been in a fight?"

"Just with you," I laughed. He looked solemn.

"Why you gotta throw that in my face?"

"I'm sorry. I didn't mean any harm."

He glanced at me with cutting eyes.

"It's okay. Just don't do that shit again. Anybody ever hurt you like they did to me in the foster homes?" he asked, looking down like he didn't want to make eye contact while talking about those hurtful memories.

Just you, I wanted to say again. But, that would change the mood, start another argument. Also, it wasn't totally true.

"Yeah. Not my family. Except, you know, whoopings from Mama Lena. Everybody got whoopings, so that doesn't count."

I recalled the red welts that swelled on my abdomen, thighs, butt, and legs from Mama Lena's leather belt when Daddy would bring me home. *Stay yo' ass in the house,* Mama Lena would yell, the belt stinging my skin with each word. *Wandering off with some crackhead like you ain't got no Goddamn sense.* My daddy ain't no crackhead, I wanted to say. I didn't want to make it worse, though, so I stayed silent, letting my tears fall until she got tired and went to her room to rest. When I was sure she wasn't coming back, I'd go to Mother's room and lay in her arms to cry.

I went back to answering Tev's question, my mouth in a straight line now.

"I come from a good family. Boys, though - boys hurt me sometimes."

"Like what?"

"Like, they took it. I didn't wanna do it and they took it."

"Raped you? That's fucked up. I'll beat those niggas' asses!"

"Well, now I got you to protect me, so I'm always gonna be safe," I replied, pressing my lips to his.

"That's right!" he replied. "Long as you love me, never fuck over me, and never leave me, I will always protect you."

I guess that was harder than it sounded. He thought I was "fucking over" him often, although I wanted no one but him. At first, when he would show up at my job and sit in the corner watching me wait tables, I felt flattered. I'd bring him free coffees and desserts and smoke cigarettes with him on my breaks. But sometimes, the male customers would flirt. After the second time he got loud threatening to whoop somebody's ass, my manager told me if Tev came back to the restaurant, he'd call the police and I'd be fired.

"That nigga couldn't wait to get me out of there, huh?" Tev asked when I got home that night.

"I mean, you... you can't be doing that. You gotta control your temper."

"Control my temper? Because I was checking dudes trying to fuck my girl? So, I'm supposed to be cool with that?"

"No. I'm just saying maybe there's a different way to handle it."

"Or maybe, you wanted them too. Or maybe, you fucking the manager. You need to quit that motherfucking job if I can't even come check on you."

"We need the money."

"I just got that new DVD burner. You can come with me to the mall and sell out the parking lot."

"I'm not really trying to sell no bootleg DVDs at the mall, Tev. I have a job already, and I almost lost it today because you came up there tripping. You just need to control your temper."

"No, you need to control your motherfucking mouth, bitch!"

He jumped from the chair where he was sitting in the corner and pushed me down onto the bed with his hands wrapped tight against my neck and his knee pressing down against my thighs.

"And you need to control your motherfucking pussy! I saw how that nigga was looking at you today. Manager, my ass. Ya'll be alone in the back and shit, huh?"

"I can't breathe, Tev," I struggled to say. Everything was getting hazy.

"I can't breathe, Tev," he mocked in a whining voice. "I'll kill you before I let you make a fucking joke out of me!"

"Please, stop," I stammered, tears running down the sides of my face. "I think I'm pregnant."

"What?" he stepped back, immediately releasing the grip.

"My period is a week late," I rubbed my neck as I spoke. "I didn't want to tell you until I took a test to be sure."

"Ah shit, baby, that changes everything. I'm so sorry."

He sat beside me and wrapped his arms around me. My body naturally flinched, but he held on tighter, kissing my face and neck.

"I'm so sorry. I do need to control my temper. I'll change. I'll go to anger management classes. Whatever it takes. I'm so, so sorry."

He kissed me between every few words, and as I looked in his eyes, I saw that he was sincere. I returned his kisses. He removed my uniform, kissing and apologizing until we were wound in the passion of lovemaking. No use in splitting up now. We were about to be a family. We could make it work.

It didn't work, though. It got worse as my pregnancy progressed. Since I didn't quit my job, Tev was still suspicious that I was cheating on him. Almost every week, I was a "lying bitch" or a "trifling ass hoe". He'd walk out at times. Other times, he'd push me against the wall or the bed before walking away.

Then, on the worst night, he decided he didn't want a baby by a "bitch who was going to leave anyway" and shoved me onto the floor in the corner, kicking me repeatedly in the chest and stomach. As usual, he left the house when his anger had been released as my pain. I crawled to the house phone and called my mom.

"Why didn't you call an ambulance?" she asked after an hour of silence.

I was lying in the hospital bed waiting on the results of the tests the doctor had run to see if my baby had survived.

"I don't know. I didn't want them judging me. I'm so stupid." My hands over my face, I broke into the tears I'd been holding back the whole night.

"You're not stupid," she replied, placing her hand on my leg. "You've always been smart."

She paused before continuing.

"But do you really wanna live like this? All your life?"

In that moment, I finally felt a real connection with my mother. It was like she was a human being and not a ghost.

"You're right," I responded, wiping my face on my hospital gown. "I gotta get away."

"I'll help you."

When the doctor came back in and said my baby had survived, I knew I couldn't go home. Mama was working now, had gone to school to be a pharmacist. She had a nice apartment where she let me stay and get on my feet for a few months without working so I could finish out my pregnancy. Once Joseph, my baby boy, was two months old, I told Mama I wanted to move to Florida. She wasn't happy about it, but Tev had been calling and showing up demanding to see Joseph more and more often. In those moments, I'd give in to the guilt of not wanting to keep him from seeing his child.

"So, you found somebody else?" he accused with a glare as he gently held the child he'd tried so hard to end.

I was always timid during our visitations because I feared if I said the wrong thing, he'd hurt me again. He seemed to be a good father as far as the way he treated Joseph, but as long as I was within reach, I felt powerless to him.

After finding another waitressing position online, Joseph and I made the trip to Tallahassee, Florida that month - a huge change. My friend Felicia from high school lived there and let us crash with her until I could afford my own place. Tev was angry initially, but then stopped calling altogether and wouldn't answer the phone when I called to let Joseph hear his voice. I wanted him to understand that I didn't want things to be this way - I just wanted to feel safe.

"You think I would hurt my child?"

"No, I think you would hurt me again."

"You think this doesn't hurt? You leaving and going who the fuck knows where with my baby?"

"I told you, I'm in Florida. I didn't mean to hurt you."

"You say that a lot, but you just keep doing it. You're the fucking worst. I never imagined I'd bring a son into the world with someone like you."

That's how our conversations went until my rebuttals would make him angry enough to go off the handle or hang up. It was always draining. But Joseph - Joseph was a happy baby and I wanted him to stay that way.

Time passed and I got promoted, starting making enough money to take night classes. I was going to be a teacher. I didn't know much, I guess, but I wanted to share what I did know with those who needed to learn.

My journey in Tallahassee involved a few boyfriends, none of whom wanted to be a father to Joseph. And Daddy was out of jail now, but our phone conversations still felt dry and forced. He'd say, "I love you," but I couldn't feel it. *Everything* was different.

As I continued my studies to be a teacher, I read more books on my own, too. Books about great people, history, religions, health, and spirituality. This search for knowledge felt like a new drug. It was the same pursuit for the missing piece. I was getting closer, I knew it.

I changed my diet and cut off my perm. Started going to yoga classes. I even applied for scholarships to go see the world. Couldn't limit myself. If there was more, I was going to find it.

Since things had cooled down, I transferred to a school back in Texas so Mama could help with Joseph while I volunteered to teach in Cameroon, helped women start businesses in Dominican Republic, planted trees in India. The bright colors, the fragrant smells, the savory flavors, the vast array of people - my world was becoming so much bigger. I felt I truly had something to offer Joseph and my future students.

My grades were stellar. I stopped working entirely and became an on-campus leader, running actions to end sweatshops and fight injustices while I lived with Mama. Tev wasn't an issue anymore; he was in jail for trying to kill another woman who was stupid enough to love him.

Speaking of love, I wanted more than anything to become close to my father again. Maybe Tev was a way of my filling the hole in my heart from Daddy not being around. I needed to go straight to the source and fix the relationship with my father. We began talking often and the flame of love re-ignited.

He told me stories about his prison days and how lonely he felt. I could relate since I felt lonely when he was gone too. We drew pictures together like we did sometimes when I was a little girl. Other times, he'd call me when he had too much to drink and ask me to come sit with him. I'd drive across town and listen to him complain about this or that girlfriend all night. He'd ask for money and I'd give him whatever I could out of my financial aid return I'd saved for my expenses. It wasn't perfect - he wasn't perfect - but, he was my daddy. I wish I'd never kept searching though.

CHAPTER 5

Seek and you shall find, that's what the Bible says. Christianity - I'd left it in Florida with pork, chicken, and red meat. However, this saying is truth. A friend invited me to a spiritual ceremony, something with plants. Ayahuasca, they called it. It sounded like Aya-Waska. I'd tried every drug except the ones daddy abused, so I wasn't afraid. We sat in a circle around an altar of fruit, candles, and pictures of the deceased. We sang and prayed. And then, we drank a bitter green liquid that tasted like Nyquil mixed with spinach.

At first, nothing was different. I saw the serene faces of the group, their white linen shirts and dresses. Then, everything was blurry like when a date I'd met in a phone chat room slipped something in my drink. I blinked fast, trying to clear the fog. As my vision clarified, I was in an all white room, that went out forever in every direction. I remembered this room from somewhere - I couldn't place it. A bright light tinted with purple emerged from thin air and spoke to me.

"Daughter. Thank you for coming. It's time for the next step. I'm sorry."

I didn't understand why this deep voice called me daughter, but it felt right. I also felt like I'd heard apologies from it before, too many apologies.

"Sorry for what?"

"Your father. Did he hurt you?"

He asked in a tone that suggested he already had an answer, like when high school teachers used to ask me, "Are you high?", "Have you been smoking?". Their concerned stares revealed they knew the truth by observing my drooping eyes and smelling the pungent traces on my skin. Still, I'd answer, "No, I'm just tired." I couldn't lie to this voice though. I thought back; no, my father had only ever been loving. Not perfect, but loving.

"No," I replied. "Why would you ask that?"

"Your father. Did he hurt you?" the voice repeated.

"No. I said no."

"Your father. Did he hurt you?"

"No! Stop asking me that!" My chest was pounding now and I felt cold sweat on my skin.

"Your father. Did he hurt you?"

"Stop! My father loves me! He would never…", but before I could finish, the room went dark.

I was back in one of the houses Daddy and I frequented. Daddy was face to face with me, his breath bitter in my nostrils.

"You're my little woman. My little wife. Ain't that right?" he said.

"Yes," I replied, feeling that wife was the highest compliment a girl or woman could receive. Wife meant a man loved you forever, til' death do ya'll part, just like in the movies.

"Daddy not gone hurt you. Daddy would never hurt you."

"I know."

And it didn't hurt at first. His mouth didn't hurt my skin. His fingers hurt a little, like a doctor giving me a shot before giving me a bandaid and a lollipop. Then, he did hurt me.

"Daddy, stop! That hurts!" I yelled, seeing blood pooling underneath my bottom as he moved in a way I didn't understand.

"Daddy would never hurt you. Daddy loves you. And you the only one who loves Daddy."

My tears and screams didn't stop him and my hands weren't strong enough to push him away.

What kind of dream was this? This was sick and horrible. Why did I ever come to this ceremony? I should have stayed home and smoked a blunt.

The darkness dissipated and I was in the white room again. The light was present.

"I'm so sorry," it said.

"What the fuck was that?"

"You can't complete your mission unless you know the truth. I'm so sorry."

"Mission, what mission. What the FUCK was that?"

My breath came in dense heaves and my face was wet, but I couldn't feel the tears emerging from my eyes.

"Your father..."

"I said, my father NEVER hurt me! Daddy would NEVER hurt me! He loves me!"

"It's time to remember. The Awakening is near. Be brave. Be strong."

"He LOVES me!"

"Remember. He doesn't know how to love. You must teach. You must show the way, daughter."

"Leave me alone!"

"You are a warrior. Remember that. A warrior of love and light. I love you. Your mother loves you. We are always with you."

The white room faded and I was in the small room with the altar. A Latino woman waved burning sage around me, whispering, "Shhh.... Shhh... it's okay. You're okay."

"My father..." I cried, my chest bursting with pain like fire.

"It's okay. Let it out."

"He... he... he hurt me," I wailed, vomiting into a waiting bucket. Everything within me emptied. Not just the food I'd eaten earlier - but my pain, my memories. Memories of every boy that had hurt me came rushing back, projecting into the bucket. Then, memories of my father. Not just in the house, but sitting in his lap in a car with no wheels, hidden behind a house. Walking through the woods, his hands on me in a way that no man should ever touch his daughter. The memories pushed more and more out of me and into the bucket, until nothing came out but green, sour bile.

"Mama..." I began. I was back at home with Mama and Joseph. He was in his room napping. He was five years old now. I was almost done with my teaching degree. This was meant to be one of the happiest times in my life.

"Yes?"

"I'm going crazy. Never mind." I couldn't tell her about the plant ceremony. She wouldn't understand. She'd think I was using drugs. She'd think I was just like my father. She'd kick me out...

"You want a Xanax?" she laughed, studying the stress lines on my face. I knew she was joking. We joked a lot about how since she was a pharmacist, she could get us all the pills we wanted and we could start a million dollar hustle.

"No," I laughed nervously. I had to say something. I would tell her they were dreams. "I've been having these dreams..."

"Yes?" Her face perked with curiosity. She believed in prophetic dreams and visions.

"These dreams about daddy... hurting me. Being inappropriate." I began to speak more quickly, so I wouldn't lose courage. "We were in those crack houses. Another time, we were in a green car. An old school type car. I know it's silly. I don't even remember Daddy having a green car." I had lost my confidence.

"He had a green Eldorado when you were five. What happened in the Eldorado?"

"He was touching me. And other things. And then we were in the woods..."

"I remember when he took you into the woods. I came out the club and saw him walking away with you and tried to run after him, but ya'll were too far away. Don't know what I coulda done anyway. I called the police..."

"You knew something was going on?" I was shocked. Tears started to well up again.

"I didn't know for sure, but I knew something wasn't right. Him taking you like that. I called the police, but they wouldn't do nothing 'cause that was yo' daddy. He had as much right to you as me."

"He said things in the dream. Called me his little woman. His little wife. Said I was the only one who loved him."

"Yes, he said some things like that to me about you too when he brought you back and we was arguing. Asked me why I was trying to keep him away from the only one who loved him. I talked to my pastor about it and he said sometimes when the man and the woman not getting along, the man tries to replace the wife with the daughter." She looked down, not making eye contact.

"Wow."

"I didn't know that he would... I never thought he would actually take it that far, but I know that your dream was not a dream. Those was memories."

I saw the tears in her eyes.

"I'm so sorry I couldn't protect you. You should never... no child should ever... I'm going to go take a walk. I need some time, I'm sorry."

Her breath was coming rapidly now like the dark truth was setting in. As hard as this was for her, I couldn't imagine her pain, knowing that the man she'd chosen to love would do this to their child. And who knew? Maybe other children.

When Mama came back, her face was swollen like she'd been crying, but it was dry now. She spoke with a stoic look, her eyes on the floor instead of on mine. She told me about how she was just a girl when they met, only 14 years old, and he was a grown man. Yet, she'd never thought about it as troubling until now. How he made her feel safe and loved after she'd been molested by Mama's Lena's husband, my Paw Paw. Daddy had given her his whole check every payday to pay the bills and then buy what she wanted. She was able to get out of the house and away from my grandma, who didn't believe Paw Paw had touched her. Everything had been good except he fought her sometimes. When my sisters and I were born, he got into smoking crack and the fighting got worse. He threatened to kill her and she felt like he would. That's when she came back to live with Mama Lena. Her spirit was broken by then, with three children at the age of 21, her life a cycle of tragedy.

"But I tried to protect you. I called the police..." her tears came again now. "It wasn't enough. I didn't do enough. I'm so sorry."

"It's okay, Mama. I understand. You tried your best," I comforted her, hugging her tight. It seemed I should be angry. I wanted to be mad at her for not doing more, but I couldn't muster up any anger. I only felt love. I was sorry for hurting her by bringing out the truth and more sorry that she had to go through all of this in her life. When would she get to be happy? Maybe now that the truth was out, she could get to a clear space with time.

"You mad at me?" she asked.

"No, I don't feel mad. What I feel is... What's the word I'm looking for? Compassion. I feel compassion for you. I wish all this bad stuff never happened to you. You didn't deserve it."

She cried harder.

"How could you be worried about me after what he did to you? I messed up. I didn't keep you safe. How can you love me? I don't deserve love."

"Oh, you deserve so much love. More love than you've gotten in your life. If I can give you a little bit of that, I'll be so grateful."

"You don't hate me?" she cried.

"I could never, never hate you. We in the same boat, Mama. We were both victims. You didn't really know and like you said, even if you did, how could you have stopped him short of killing him?

"Maybe..."

"No, Mama. That would have been real bad."

"You don't want him dead?"

She looked confused.

"No. I don't understand how he could do that to me or why he would do it, but I wish no harm on him. I pray for his healing."

"You are... an angel. You got to be. How could God bless me with an angel like you?"

"Maybe we're both angels, just trying to make a way," I replied, hugging her again. "Angels who need Xanax."

We burst into laughter.

CHAPTER 6

"You are a channel for light. You are a vessel for light. You bring light to the darkest places," a beautiful female voice said in a voice sweet like song.

I was back in the white room. I knew I was asleep now. How did I end up back here? Was the ayahuasca still in me?

"The veil has been broken, daughter. I am so happy that you can see me again. I've never left your side. Please know that," she said. Her cocoa face was like mine, her eyes almond shaped like mine too. She wore a blue hooded cloak, with the hood down on her shoulders. Her head was shaved, but there was no denying her femininity. She was like... the embodiment of femininity.

"This darkness. You now see your father's darkness. Be encouraged. You are light. The darkest places need the brightest light."

She embraced me and I felt the deep pain rising from my body as if she was absorbing it.

"I'm dreaming. This is a dream, right?" I asked, feeling her warmth in a way I'd never felt in a dream.

"A dream within a dream. The only reality is love."

I jolted awake, laying in my bed with Joseph asleep in my arms. Blinking and looking around the room, I saw her standing in the corner watching us.

"I am always here," she said, before fading away.

Now, I knew I was crazy.

After getting dressed, I contemplated calling my father. What would I say to him? He would surely deny any wrongdoing. I couldn't bear to hear him lie and comfort me, telling me he loved me when I knew the truth. I was committed to forgiveness, but I couldn't talk to him. Not yet. It was too soon.

"We need to talk," Mama said, walking in as I scrambled tofu for breakfast.

"All ears," I replied, forcing a smile, although I was still concerned about how to bring this to my father and confused about the woman from my dream who appeared in my room.

"No, not me and you. We need to talk to Jaylen. She's had Jasmine at your daddy's house almost every weekend..."

Jaylen was my 19-year-old niece and Jasmine was her gorgeous 4-year-old daughter.

"Mama, I don't think that's necessary. Daddy was on crack when all this happened. He's clean now."

"He wasn't on crack when we met and when you think about it, I was just a girl too. He was a grown man."

My stomach knotted and I lost my appetite. He couldn't....

"I guess it won't hurt to talk," I replied in a near whisper. Mama was the strong one now. I'd told her all I knew, but I felt a stagnating fear when I thought about my whole family knowing what happened. What would they think of Daddy? What would they think of me?

It wasn't your fault, a voice inside my head said. It was the woman in blue cloak's melodic voice. How was she in my mind? *Be encouraged*, she continued. *Be brave. Be strong*, the male voice I'd heard in the white room said. I was hearing things. I shook my head.

"Are you saying no?" Mama asked, misinterpreting my movement.

"No, it's fine. I'm sorry," I responded, feeling ashamed that she'd seen me in that moment. "Let's talk to her."

We called Jaylen and told her the situation on speakerphone. She was silent.

"We would have come in person, but it's important you talk to your daughter now," Mama instructed, stronger than I'd ever seen her. "Ask her if anyone has ever touched her on her... private places."

"Okay, I guess. I'll ask her." Jaylen seemed to be in shock.

Less than an hour later, as I watched cartoons with Joseph, I saw Jaylen's name on my phone. *I'm sure everything's fine*, I thought, answering the call.

"She said yes," Jaylen said in a tear-strained voice. "She said... he touched her and gave her candy long as she wouldn't say nothing. I can't believe this shit!"

I didn't know what to say to her. I was just as shocked and appalled. Daddy wasn't just on crack; he was a pedophile and the shit hadn't stopped.

"What are we going to do?" I asked my mama after getting off the phone with Jaylen.

"What can we do?" she responded, staring at me blankly like she was the ghostly woman at my grandmother's house again.

"We have to stop him," I replied, feeling like it was obvious.

"I will... I will pray about it," she said in a monotone voice, packing up her things for work and walking out the door.

This wasn't a prayer situation. We needed to do something actively to stop him. Could I just call the police? I couldn't imagine calling the police on my father. This was like a bad dream. I remembered all the laughter we shared as I rode on his shoulders each time he lifted me away for another adventure. In my memories up until now, these had been the happiest days. But, it wasn't real. The parts left out were the pieces most important now.

When I was 9, he was "doing good", Mama Lena said. He had stopped smoking crack, although he was still selling it. At that time, Mama Lena was not innocent either, so she did not judge his position. In fact, she was the one cooking the crack for him and others to sell. Her club had been closed down due to several murders that happened on the property following drunken fights and she did not want to sacrifice her lifestyle. Although we were never rich, the one thing Mama Lena could not stand to be was poor.

I knew that she had grown up picking cotton like her mother and I could not imagine what that meant as far as how she had to live day-to-day. When I was born, she was already a businesswoman, doing whatever was necessary to stay driving the nicest cars and wearing the most top-of-the-line clothing while providing for me, my sisters, my mama, and my great grandmother. We never had to go a day hungry or naked.

At that time, when I was 9, my father could knock on the door and she would *let him* drive away with me and my sisters. They didn't fight anymore.

He would take us to a public pool in the White neighborhood across the track.

"Arms out front. Now, kick your legs, baby. Kick your legs! There you go! You got it!" he encouraged with a smile as I splashed water in every direction doing a rough doggy paddle.

We would swim until we were exhausted and then order pizzas and bask in the sun.

When I was 10, we spent much of our time together drawing. He was the greatest artist I'd ever known. I'd been to museums on school field trips and seen the splashes of colorful paint that passed off as great art, but could they draw a cowboy on a horse in perfect detail in less than 10 minutes? Daddy was an artistic genius, doing work with a pencil or even a pen that I could never emulate.

"Those is cartoon eyes, baby; those not *real* eyes. Look at my eyes. Now, draw what you see."

I carefully penciled the almond shape of his shining eyes, taking my time to shade the fine lines and circle in the pupils.

"Now, *those* is real eyes!" he affirmed when I finally got it right.

Every day that I spent with my father was special. We would eat ice cream together as he told jokes, or he'd take me out to the front yard and teach me to build a dog house from two by fours for the stray dogs I fed, or he'd say, "Go put on some britches!", and teach me to cut the lawn with a gas-powered push mower. There was never a time when we were together when he'd stare at me blankly like my mother. I never felt the tension that any wrong move would result with a lashing from a leather belt like when I was with Mama Lena.

When I was 11 and his business was going really well, he would bring me and my sisters each a crisp twenty dollar bill every Friday and drop us off at the movie theater. We would stock up on nachos and sour candies at the snack bar and then movie hop all day.

When he came to pick us up, he didn't ask us suspicious questions about what movies we'd seen or if we had boys with us like Mama Lena; he would only ask if we had fun. Sometimes, he would come inside and play in the arcade with us for hours before we left.

Because of him, I was the top shooter in every alien hunting game ever created.

I wished this could all just go away. But, I knew it wouldn't go away on its own. Though I knew the truth, it was not enough. It was more important to accept it and to act on it.

Taking a deep breath, I searched online on my phone for 'what to do when a child has been touched. The child abuse hotline phone number popped up. I dialed it, but did not push send. Instead, I went back to my room and found a pen and paper. Joseph was still sleeping. I shut the door and went to lie in my mother's room, in her bed, putting pen to paper.

My body is not a temple, but

A haunted house,

Holding the ghosts of your touch,

Sheltering the flames of your kiss,

Sheltering the demons

> *Of your forbidden fantasies;*

My wounds, unhealed, part and bleed,

Under realization that even now,

You desire to consume innocence;

My beliefs about you - lies,

My love for you - poisoned,

My desires to heal you - worthless,

You are who you are...

My killer,

My betrayer,

My father,

My love for you is a noose,

Carrying my heart to a slow and painful death.

As I wrote, tears spotted the page, rendering the straight lines into dispersed pools of blue ink.

"Daddy!" I cried out, my chest heaving with hot air as I cried like a little girl who had just seen her loving father murdered before her eyes. Pulling the blanket over my head, I mourned for what must have been an hour before I felt that I could maybe dial the number.

"You the only one who love me. You the only one who never turned against me and won't never hurt me."

My father's words repeated again and again in my mind, stagnating my finger. In my heart, I'd promised to never hurt him, to never turn on him.

Was there any way that I could stand by his side now? No, he'd gone too far. To stand by him would be to corroborate in other little girls being asked to open their bodies like grown women to a man they thought of as "family". To stand by him would transform me from a victim to a villain. There was only one path to victory, the path I dreaded most. I pressed send.

"Hello, I'd like to report the abuse of child."

After collecting my basic information, the woman on the other end of the line came back to the purpose of our call.

"Okay, who would you like to report?"

"My father," I said, feeling that some primal cord had been cut with those two words. I was no longer his confidant; I was a traitor. While it hurt like being split from a siamese twin, somehow, I felt free.

CHAPTER 7

Now that everything was different, I could never be the same. It was months later, and my father had still not been arrested. I also hadn't spoken to him, despite his phone calls and texts. He messaged me as if nothing had changed - "Hey baby, I miss you. Call me. I love you." What kind of fantasy world was he living in? I guess, a fantasy world where a man could violate his own daughter and his own granddaughter and still walk the streets free.

It didn't bother me the most that he wasn't incarcerated. My goal wasn't to punish my father; it was to protect Jasmine and other girls from him. His house was a magnet for children who needed babysitting. He was the jovial grandpa with a home full of snacks, candy, games, and laughter. Although we had convinced Jaylen not to take Jasmine there initially, now that Daddy hadn't been arrested, other family members were putting pressure on her to bring her back around him.

"That's her grandpa; he would never do that. That baby lying. She ain't but four. Children lie," my sister Janae, Jaylen's mom, told her.

It wasn't long before Janae stopped trying to make a case and just took Jasmine to see Daddy.

"I'm her mama! I get to make the decisions!" Jaylen pleaded.

"And I'm yo' mama! So, *I* make the fucking decisions!" Janae replied.

Janae's loyalty to Daddy was terrifying. I asked Mama about it and she admitted that while she had been unsure as to whether Daddy would have done anything to me since I was so young when he took him, she feared him being around Janae, who was five years older. When we were kids, and even now, Janae was gorgeous. As a child, I was never complimented for my looks. With a round, deep chocolate face and short, kinky hair, I was at the end of more "You so black" jokes than I could recall.

"You so black, yo' blood type is burnt."

"You so black, when you go to school, you blend in with the chalkboard."

"You so black, you drink water and pee coffee."

"You so black, yo' pictures look like ultrasounds."

"You so black, lightning bugs follow you in the daytime."

"You so black, when God made you, He said, damn, I burnt one."

But Janae, she was the apple of everyone's eyes. With caramel skin and hair down to the middle of her back, she was called pretty so often, it was like her nickname. Although she was still beautiful, her life had not moved forward any farther than when she was in her teen years. Lacking the drive or consistency to work, she lived with Jaylen in her section 8 apartment, smoking weed and playing video games all day or entertaining male company. She did not behave like a mother; she behaved like a roommate. Yet, she ordered Jaylen around like Jaylen was living off her.

My powerlessness to protect anyone from my father or resolve my own grief about all this new, difficult information was turning into depression. I had been depressed before. When Joseph was about 7 months old and Tev was fighting on me worse than ever, before I felt strong enough to leave, I felt absolutely hopeless. My love for Tev was a ball and chain and I was a failure as a mother and a person for not being able to break it. How could I call myself a mother when I couldn't even protect myself and my son? I'd be waitressing for the rest of my short, desolate fucking life until Tev killed me. And if he didn't start beating Joseph's ass too, he'd raise him to be the same damn way. With these thoughts running through my head, I ate a whole bottle of pain relievers, praying they would once and for all, take away my pain.

Remembering that moment now, I recall an inner voice saying something like, "the exit is blocked", before I threw up all that I had consumed. For the rest of the night, I had a terrible stomach ache. The next day, I woke up and felt fine. That was when I decided I had to leave. If I couldn't take the easy way out, I had to take the hard way. I had to get my courage together and start a new life.

That's what I needed now, too, to save me from this impending depression. A new life. I'd be graduating with my Bachelor's Degree in Education in a week. I wasn't going to stay here and teach full-time while watching my family implode. Fuck that. I had a couple of income tax refunds saved up - I was leaving. If I couldn't save my family, I'd save someone somewhere else. I'd helped women and children all over the world on my study abroad trips. Every time a foreign face smiled and said, "thank you", I felt useful, powerful, like I was making a difference. After some quick research online, I found an opportunity.

"Mama, I'm moving to Costa Rica," I stated when my mother got home.

"You taking Joseph?"

"Yes, I found a school to volunteer at and he can go to school there. After a while, I'll find a teaching job to support myself."

"You gone have to speak Spanish?" she asked, not seeming surprised at my decision.

"Yes. You know I learned Spanish waitressing, though; so that's no problem."

"Okay. When you leaving?"

I couldn't be sure, but there seemed to be some relief in her eyes, like she was glad I was getting away from all this. Jaylen was not as calm when I broke the news to her.

"No! You can't leave! What if Papa does something to Jasmine? I believe her. She ain't no lying child. My mama just keep taking her over there and I can't stop it. If he... I would have to... I'd have to kill him."

"Then you'd go to prison, throw your life away," I replied, not sure what else to say.

"I don't give a fuck! I love my daughter. I'll kill everybody, him, my mama - everybody - to protect her if I have to!" I could hear the tears in her voice.

"There has to be something else we can do."

"Ain't nothing else! They just gotta die!"

This was getting out of control. I'd opened this can of worms; it couldn't end with a double homicide and my niece in prison. There had to be another way.

"No, Jaylen. I'll take her. I'll take Jasmine with me to Costa Rica."

"Yes! That's a great idea! What do I need to do? We can't tell my mama. I'll pack Jasmine a bag right now. When you leaving?" Her excitement surprised me; I knew how much she loved her daughter. But, love will make you do crazy things like suffering the pain of missing your baby every day if you know it will keep her out of harm's way.

"I'm leaving in three weeks. I will come get you and we'll talk about everything we need to do to get ready."

It was surprisingly easy to get Jasmine's passport and plane ticket ready with ours since her father, like Joseph's, hadn't signed the birth certificate. Everything was unfolding quickly in a new direction. There was one thing I still needed to do before I left American soil though - talk to my father. It would take courage and patience. I didn't know that I was ready to hear anything that he had to say. But, I couldn't leave things without some type of closure.

"Hello?"

"Hey, baby! I missed you so much. You been busy with school?"

"Yes." If only it were that simple. I took a deep breath. "That's not why I haven't been calling, though. I need to talk to you about something."

I didn't want to start the conversation with what happened to Jasmine. What he did to Jasmine. I needed to talk to him about what happened, what he *did,* to me.

"Daddy, you remember when I was little, when you used to take me?"

"Yeah, baby. You were a fat, lil' thang, but still wanted to ride on my shoulders. I still got back problems from that," he laughed. His laugh was rich and hearty. It could warm the heart of a snowman.

"Well, think back to that time. Did anything ever happen... did anyone ever *touch* me?"

My courage wasn't quite strong enough to ask him if he did it. To get him to admit it. Not yet.

"Touch you like what?"

"Touch me in a sexual way."

He was silent for a few moments.

"Sexual? You were just a baby. Now, when you was 'bout 13 or 14, I think you started having sex. I was at the house one day and saw you sneakin' out the window, probably to see some lil' snot-nosed boy. You remember I talked to you about that."

"I'm not talking about when I was a teenager."

"You was just kind of fast. I knew it when you started puttin' on lipstick. You was smart though, always made good grades, so I just prayed about it. Hadn't never whooped you before, didn't wanna start."

"Daddy, I'm not talking about that. I'm talking about when you used to take me. Was I touched in a sexual way?"

"Honestly, baby, I don't remember. That was a long time ago. All I can tell you is that you a strong woman now. Whatever happened, it made you stronger."

"Daddy..."

"I don't know why you even bringing this to me. Yo' mama put you up to this? You know the doctor diagnosed me with cancer? In my prostate. Stage three. I been getting chemo."

"I'm sorry to hear that."

"I might not have long. Don't put this on me now. My heart can't take it. How I'm 'posed to remember something from twenty something years ago? You turned out the best out of all yo' sisters. You know what it say in the bible. The last shall be the first. You the youngest and you the best."

"You didn't answer my question."

"That's because I don't know! All I know is I love you. If that ain't enough, I'm sorry. That's what you want me to say? I'm sorry. I'm *sorry*, baby. All I want is to see you. When you gone come see me again? I miss you and my boy. You act like you forgot about yo' daddy now that you in school. Just like yo' mama. I'm dying and all you can think about is the past."

"This is not about you."

"Then who it's about? Who phone you calling? I know yo' mama turned you against me. She got child protective services calling my house talkin' about something with Jasmine, like I would *ever*... Tell you the truth, that child fast just like her mama. I was laying on the floor to help my back pain and she come crawling on top of me and start hunching like a woman. I pushed her off me and she did it again. Her mama must be over there playin' rodeo with some lil' snot-nosed niggas in front of that baby. Yo' mama need to call them people on her, not me!"

It felt like we were going in every direction but the truth. Somehow, he had managed to make himself the victim and all of us the ones in the wrong. My head was spinning and I felt anger burning in my chest.

"Are you gone come see me before I die?" he continued. "I got another chemo treatment next week and I gotta get back surgery. Pray for me, baby. I don't know why God see fit for me to suffer like this. But you remember the story of Job. God tests us before doubling our blessings..."

I hung up. I couldn't hear any more of this. A minute later, I received a text from him - "The call dropped. Must be the service on my end. I love you."

I love you too, I thought, but I couldn't type it. If I couldn't be anything else, I'd be a mirror to show him the wrongdoing he refused to see. If I couldn't hold him back from hurting children, I'd at least withhold the three words I've given him so freely for my whole life. My love for him was so real, so deep, I knew that I couldn't even stay angry. What I could do was stay away.

CHAPTER 8

We arrived in Costa Rica without a single obstacle. At first, everything was smooth and I was at peace. I would teach in the mornings while Joseph and Jasmine learned in the classroom next door. They were learning Spanish quickly. In the afternoons, we'd grab a few items from the market and I'd go to our small apartment provided with the volunteer program and cook a healthy dinner. Nights, I'd read to them and then we would all sleep. It was a simple routine. I felt I could repeat this routine for the rest of my life; it was so peaceful.

But, it wasn't long before things became different again. It started with a girl in my class - Mariana. She ran a terrible fever during class and had to be picked up by her mother. The next morning, she was not at school. I asked about her and was told she was in the hospital and things were quickly worsening. Some kind of virus, they said. She probably wouldn't live.

I couldn't bear to think that I'd never see this sweet girl with the snaggle-toothed smile again. After school, I dropped Joseph and Jasmine with one of the nice abuelas that looked after volunteers' children and caught a taxi to the hospital. Mariana was there, sweating and pale, her mother holding her little hand. *Los siento*, I said to her mother. *I'm so sorry.*

In that moment, I heard the melodic voice of the blue-cloaked woman in my mind. *Lay your hands on her.* It seemed right, so I didn't question it. *Allow the light to flow through you.* I felt the light, a hot energy flowing through my palms.

"You pray for my daughter?" her mother said in broken English.

"Yes," I replied, though I wasn't sure prayer was what was happening.

"God heal my daughter?"

"Yes," I responded again, the heat in my hands burning uncomfortably.

Before my eyes, the color began returning to the girl's sleeping face. With her eyes still closed, she smiled. I knew that she was healed.

"Thank you, Jesus!" her mother cried, looking up to sky with watery eyes.

Leave now, daughter. You've done enough. Again, I followed the voice without question.

I picked up the children and went home and cooked dinner, staying with the routine. The next morning, Mariana was back in her desk. She was smiling and healthy. *Un miracle,* she told the other teachers when they asked. *Jesus healed me.* Although I wasn't religious anymore, I wanted to believe that she was right. Yet, Jesus wasn't in that room. It was just me, her mother, and the voice inside my head. What really took place, I didn't understand.

Then, it happened again. This time, it was the abuela who babysat for me. *She's so sick,* the villagers said in Spanish. *She doesn't have long.* We walked to her house and as the children played in the yard, I sat in a chair by the abuela's bedside.

"Thank you for coming. My family is out today and I don't want to be alone," she said to me in Spanish.

"Of course. You have been so kind to me."

I didn't know how I got this power and how exactly to use it, but it had healed Mariana. Wanting more than anything to give the abuela the same gift, I waited. There was no voice, no instruction. *Please help me,* I whispered, praying to the blue-cloaked woman who called me daughter. *Thank you for asking for help*, she responded, within my thoughts. *I didn't ask last time,* I responded silently. *You didn't know to ask*, she replied. *How do I heal this woman?* I asked. *Ask her about her husband,* she answered.

"Has your husband come to visit?" I inquired.

"Oh no, my husband..." she stopped as tears ran down her age-worn cheeks, "My husband left me all alone. He got good job. Making money. He left me and found a girl, young like my granddaughters. They living together now, husband and wife."

I was so sorry to have brought it up. *Ask her has she forgiven him?* the blue-cloaked woman said. Eager to get to the part where the abuela was healed, I followed the command.

"Have you forgiven your husband?"

"I know Jesus said to forgive, but how can I?" she responded, still crying. "He was my first love and he treat me like nothing. Throw me away."

At a loss as to what to say now, I simply listened and followed the blue-cloaked woman's instruction's again.

"Send him love. Let him go, grandmother."

"Oh, how can I?"

"For God so loved the world, he let His only son go. That couldn't have been easy. Feel God's love now, let it fill you and let your husband go. Send him love."

"I do, I do love him! I do forgive him! May God bless him with a new life and many more children. I am an old woman, so tired of this life. I am ready to go home."

As she spoke these lines, she transitioned from wailing each word to being perfectly calm. Serene.

Tell her she can go now. God is ready for her. Again, I followed the voice.

Afterwards, I left the abuela's house and completed my nightly routine. The next morning, I was told she had passed away peacefully in her sleep. I didn't understand. I needed answers. And there was only one person who could provide them.

When we arrived home, I shut myself inside my room as the children played in the front and kneeled at my bedside.

"Where are you?" I asked.

"Always with you," the woman replied, her voice clear as day like she was standing next to me. I looked around and saw no one.

"I don't see you."

"You're not ready. Last time I showed myself, you were afraid."

"Who are you?"

"I am your mother."

"I have a mother. She lives in Texas."

"She is not your mother. Your parents are not your true parents; they are souls you came to help evolve as you evolve alongside them."

"Why didn't you heal that woman?" I had so many questions about what she just shared, but right now, I wanted to know why she didn't help the abuela.

"You healed her."

"She died. I heard this morning."

"She left her body. No one ever dies."

"You healed the girl - Mariana."

"You healed her."

"Why didn't you heal the abuela?"

"When she forgave her husband, she was healed. Now, her spirit is at peace."

"But you didn't heal her body!"

"Being in a state of peace with love for all is the highest form of healing. Thank you for helping her."

"This is too much. What if Mariana had died too? I would have been devastated."

"We wouldn't have given you what you weren't ready for; so no, that would not have taken place. You were sent to those souls to realize some things about yourself."

"To realize what?"

"Your power. The God within you. You are a channel for Divine Light. Use it wisely. Be the love. Be the light."

"What if that's more than I'm ready for?"

She didn't answer. It was as if she walked away or hung up the phone on me. This was ridiculous anyway. Why was I shut in my room talking to myself? I had to be going crazy. Coming out into the kitchen, I washed my hands to make dinner for the children. I was in such a rush to get home and ask questions, I hadn't stopped at the market for fresh vegetables. Pulling a pack of noodles from the cabinet, I was startled by the brand name. "Ready now", the bright red package said in Spanish. This couldn't be a coincidence. So, this was her way of answering. I certainly didn't feel ready, but I was desperately curious to know more. If this was my power, I wanted to use it. I wanted to help people heal. This was a way my life could mean something. I would never have to feel powerless again, like I had so many times. If that meant that I was "ready now", then I guess I was.

CHAPTER 9

And as they say, when the student is ready, the teacher will appear. The next day at work, a fellow American teacher, Kiana struck up a conversation with me about the abuela who passed away.

"She lived a good life, being a good person and helping children. That's all we can strive for - to live our purpose while we're here. No matter if it seems large, small, ridiculous, mundane... no one's path is same," Kiana said, mid-conversation. I was surprised to hear someone my age speaking with such spiritual understanding and wisdom.

"Do you know your purpose, Kiana?" I asked.

"In this lifetime? To open new energetic pathways through being a trailblazer for positive change."

"That's deep. What do you mean by 'in this lifetime'? Do you think you've lived other lives?"

"Oh, I know I have. I've seen some of them. We learn from each one and they all connect."

"How many lives have you lived?"

"There is no beginning and no end. If you are interested in finding out more about your previous lives, I can help you with that."

"Really? How?" I replied, intrigued.

"Past life regression. It's like going to a therapist's office. You relax and let your past lives reveal themselves through speaking about them. If you like, I can come over later and walk you through one or a few."

"I would love that!" I affirmed.

I put the children to bed early to prepare for Kiana coming over. She brought a chair from the kitchen to sit next to my bed and guided me through some deep breathing exercises to relax and a prayer of protection.

"Remember that no matter what you see or hear inside of your mind, nothing can hurt you. First, let's practice by having you picture your favorite place. See any place that you would like and describe it to me."

"I'm in a field of green, green grass. My grandmother's yard. I'm lying on my back, feeling the soft blades pressing against my arms."

"What else do you see?"

"There's a big plum tree on my left. The plums are ready now; they're a bright orange red."

"Do you hear anything?"

"I hear the breeze stirring in my ears like a subtle ocean wave. I hear the birds chirping. It's morning, but not too early. The sky is bright blue. The grass is dry; no dew. A grasshopper just jumped onto my chest. I'm staring into its eyes. I'm smiling."

"How do you feel?"

"Very happy. Completely at peace."

"Okay, as I count down from ten, you will come out of this space."

Kiana explained to me that I would see my past lives in this way - like a video in my head. As I saw each one, I would describe it aloud to her. We began.

"Imagine yourself at the top of a white staircase," she began. "Do you feel the railing?"

"Yes."

"Now, walk down each step. How do they feel?"

"Cold and smooth. Marble." My eyes were closed and I could see the stairs clearly.

"When you get to the bottom of the steps, there is a hallway. Walk down the hallway and you will see two doors, one on the left and one on the right. Which door would you like to open?"

"The door on the left."

"Please open it and step inside."

"I'm inside."

"What do you see?"

"I'm on a balcony. I am staring into the blue sky."

"What are you wearing?"

"A beautiful white dress. The material is light and blows behind me in the wind."

"Where are you?"

"At home. This is my family's home. We live in North Africa. In Egypt."

"What do you do there?"

"I am a healer and an oracle. I help many people. I hold many ceremonies. This is my job, but I am not happy."

"Why are you unhappy?"

"This is not my own life. My family decided what I would be, what I would do. My marriage was arranged. I do not love my husband. I only love my daughter. I want her to be happy, to make her own choices."

As I continued to describe my life is Egypt, Kiana asked questions to walk me through it. We skipped to different important scenes in my life until the day that I was a spirit standing beside my body. At this point, I stepped back out into the hallway and into another door. This time, I saw a life in West Africa where I also had healing gifts that I used to help others, but I was very young. A teenager. As I was enjoying a day outdoors with my friends, an army stormed our village, tearing our families apart, taking prisoners of war. As others ran, I planted my feet firmly to fight the men, but was not victorious. They held me captive for weeks with very little food and water before handing me off to White men with brown hair who canoed me with other girls onto a large ship. The ship's bottom, where we were kept chained, was damp and cold. I was so afraid for my family. Another girl told me she had heard stories of these men from a seer; how they would make us work with no wages and force their bodies upon us. With each tale she told, I was more and more sure that I did not want this new life. When we were brought to the deck of the ship unchained to be bathed with cold ocean water, I jumped from the side into the ocean to swim back home. We were too far away. As my arms became heavy, my body sank and my spirit rose.

In another life, I was enslaved somewhere in America. We were harvesting cotton, which left cuts in my hands. There was a woman I talked to often, a friend. She was burned alive for trying to escape. I had memories of Africa that I shared with others who were captive through folktales. They loved listening to me and I loved telling stories. When I was older, I helped some to escape and then came back for others. Someone betrayed me and I was pursued. I set the plantation's house on fire before being eaten by dogs. When I set the house aflame, I did it with only words, not oil or matches. I had some type of power. I didn't understand why I didn't use my power to save myself, but Kiana told me not to try to analyze the visions, just to verbalize them.

After this last regression, we did more breathing exercises and I came out of the meditative space. She asked me what I learned from seeing these lives.

"I was powerful, gifted, and determined in each life. I was not always happy, but I had happy moments. There were many difficulties to overcome. More often than not, I put others before myself. In two of the lives, I ran away from some situation, but didn't really get away."

"Do you see any parallels between those lives and your current life?" she asked.

"I still have gifts and determination, although I don't usually feel powerful. I'm still not happy all the time. I still put others first, most of the time. And even now, I'm running. I ran to Costa Rica to start a new life, but kind of like before, I'm not really getting away. I have my niece with me to keep her safe, I still have family problems back home, and I've been having some strange experiences here similar to ones I started to have in Texas."

"Strange like what?"

"Like helping people heal in miraculous ways."

"That's not strange. That's divine. We all have gifts."

"But I'm just a normal person. I'm not supposed to be doing stuff like that."

"What is normal?"

"You know... I've had a regular ass fucked up life. If I was so special, why did I have to struggle? Why did I have to be beat up by my son's father? Why did my father... never mind."

"Why do you think these things happened?"

"I don't know. Maybe to punish me? Maybe I hurt some people in a life I didn't see?"

"We don't just go through tragedy for punishment. It can be to learn lessons, like to develop an understanding of suffering on earth."

"Why would I want to understand suffering?"

"Nelson Mandela said that our common suffering allows us to be bound through compassion and that this compassion is our hope for the future."

"Like, we can't have a better world without compassion and we can't have compassion without common suffering?" I responded.

"Exactly."

"There has to be an easier way," I laughed, wiping a tear that had flowed from my right eye.

"Well, I've heard that Earth is a school for souls to evolve; that it's not supposed to be easy."

"Then, I need a ticket to another planet," I laughed, sitting up to walk Kiana out before it got too late.

We hugged and I thanked her before she left for her apartment. I couldn't believe that I'd just seen three of my past lives. What did it all mean? I kneeled by my bed to try to reach my "mother" again.

"Mother, are you there?"

"I'm always here," I heard audibly. "Get off your knees."

I laid down under my blanket, pulling it over my head, and closed my eyes. Surprisingly, I could see a violet light under my eyelids.

"I saw some of my past lives. How long have I existed?"

"Always."

"But, what does it all mean? What do I do with this information?"

"Integrate."

"Integrate what?"

"All that you've learned. It is time for the Awakening. Use all that you've gathered to be the light now."

"How can I 'be the light'?"

"Love. There is only love."

I didn't ask any more questions because I didn't understand the answers she'd already given me. What was the point in having this connection if she sounded like a fortune cookie? Everything Kiana said made sense though. Perhaps tomorrow after work, she could help me understand.

CHAPTER 10

When I completed my classes the next day, I was quick to find Kiana before she left.

"Kiana! I feel like there are all these puzzle pieces that don't fit together into a complete picture."

"Well, how was your day, too?" she laughed, reminding me that my anxiety was making me discourteous.

"I'm sorry. I'm just more confused."

"All the answers don't come at once. Maybe you should get a reading."

"A reading? What do you mean?"

"I know someone who may able to help you. I'll walk you to her house."

As we walked with Joseph and Jasmine in tow, we laughed about our experiences in Costa Rica. We joked about the married taxi drivers flirting with us, haggling for the best prices at the market, and becoming accustomed to cold showers. After a couple miles of walking and talking, we reached a small, blue wooden house.

"Cristiana?" Kiana called from the front door. A Latino woman with her head wrapped in a white cloth and elaborate colorful beads around her neck opened the door and greeted us.

"How can I help you?" Cristiana asked in English.

"My friend needs a reading, please. I am not going to stay. I have a prior engagement."

Kiana was so kind for taking the time to walk us all the way here when she had her own plans for the afternoon. After thanking her, she left us. Cristiana sat me at a brown, wooden circular table and spread white tarot cards with varying black ink designs on the back into three rows of three. Turning them over to reveal images, she spoke.

"You are very special. A healer and seer. You are just learning your gifts."

"Is that what this card means?" I asked.

"The cards are just for show. What I share comes from beyond."

"I'm sorry. I'm listening."

"Don't apologize. Don't apologize for asking questions and don't apologize for who you are. You have a powerful mission. You are here to heal your family."

"How can I do that? That's where I feel most powerless... in helping my family."

"You are already doing it, but the biggest test will come soon. You will break generations of hurt. You will open the way for the future of your bloodline to be bright. There is much darkness."

"Yes, my father..."

"He is like... an angel. Your father."

"He's far from an angel. *Muy, muy mal.* He..."

"He has been scarred in many lifetimes. It is your job to make it right. You have come for this."

"I don't see how I can do that. He won't even admit to what he's done. I can't talk to him. I can't hear him lie anymore."

"No talk, you show him."

"Show him *how*?"

"Through forgiveness. Through love."

"I feel like I've already forgiven him. Can you tell me more about my own life - not my father, not my family, but me. I want to know about me."

"You are here for them. That is all you need to know. Heal your father."

Cristiana wouldn't tell me anything else, so I thanked her and paid her for her time. This path led to more and more confusion. Was I supposed to heal my father of cancer? How could I do that from Costa Rica? Did I need to fly back? What about Jasmine? If I healed him, would he just try to hurt more children for his own pleasure?

I didn't think he deserved healing, to be honest. Mariana, a little girl who had never hurt anyone, she deserved to be healed. The kind grandmother who chose to go "home" instead of suffering more in this life, she deserved peace. My father deserved something else. Cancer that could make him impotent - that made sense for him. Hell, if it existed - maybe he deserved that too. But healing? Health was for good people, not men that switched up like Dr. Jekyll and Mr. Hyde to use children as sex toys. I couldn't see myself helping him like that and maybe that was what she meant by forgiveness. I'd always loved my father and didn't realize until this moment that I was so angry. Now that I knew I had this power to heal others, if I was honest, I wanted to punish him through denying him that gift.

As we walked home, my anger intensified. I'd read about energy transferring, and didn't even want to hold the children's hands or cook their food with how I was feeling. I needed to release. After ordering them bean burritos from a local stand and going home, I went to my room alone to write and release. I'd heard of people writing letters and burning them to help with forgiveness. It couldn't hurt to try it for myself.

Daddy, I forgive you. I love you. I always thought I was your favorite and you were definitely my favorite person in the world. My best memories are with you...

       This wasn't helping. It wasn't honest. This anger burning within me, I was afraid to let it out. I wanted to be a good person, a good daughter. I needed to set my fear aside and write my truth.

Daddy,

I don't forgive you. Fuck you. You're dying because it's karma for all the foul shit you've done to me and other people. When I was a little girl, I trusted you and you betrayed me! How could you desire your own child? How could you say you loved me and do that to me? I don't understand that kind of evil! How could you do that to your baby daughter? I fucking hate you. You disgust me.

I go through the fucking routine and try to love you, but how can I? It's because of you that I chose a man who would hurt me. You ruined my fucking life! Then, when I try to talk to you, you make it all about you! You force me to hold in my feelings and

97

cater to yours. Well, fuck you. I'm not doing it anymore. You deserve to die. I'll cut my hands off before I use them to heal you. Burn in hell.

As I wrote, I cried deep from my stomach. What did Cristiana mean when she said my father was like an angel? He seemed more like the devil to me, but I guess according to the Bible, Lucifer was once an angel too. If you had fallen so far from the light that you created hell not just for yourself, but for others, was there anything angelic left in you? When I thought of him, I did feel light. I felt the love we shared in my childhood years. But, that was all fake. He was manipulating me through smiles and laughter to take what he wanted.

Then again, what if the love was just as real as the pain? What if the joy was as real as the darkness? I needed more information. Had he always been evil or had something changed him? This wasn't just about him. Whatever was in him, was in me. I am his daughter. If there was some poison growing and spreading in him, surely, I was infected too. Maybe healing him was the only way to save myself from a similar fate.

CHAPTER 11

I needed more answers, deeper answers, and I wasn't sure where to get them. I didn't want to go back to the psychic. Something about her approach rubbed me the wrong way. I didn't want to go to another ayahuasca ceremony and throw up until saw another realm. I just wanted straight answers. There had to be a way to get that.

Searching 'how to find spiritual answers' online, I came across many resources on lucid dreaming, divination, and meditation. Yet, one method stood out to me more than others. When I read the term 'Akashic Records', my heart pumped faster and the hair stood up on my arms. I knew this was it.

The Akashic Records were described as the records of one's complete existence, in all lifetimes, until now. Apparently, this was an actual place, in a higher dimension. And, there were guides who guarded your records and would answer any questions for you that you had about them. I saw that I could ask about any of my past lives, as well as what my contract is in my current life – like, what I signed up for before I got here.

There were directions listed for how one could access their own records on some sites. On others, people offered to access them for you for a fee. I didn't feel confident to go through my process on my own, at least not the first time, so I called up a sister with a very reasonable price and she provided the phone reading the same day.

She told me of lifetimes where I lived in Africa as a healer, as an oracle, and as a warrior. She told me of lifetimes where I was enslaved and ran away, and she told of lifetimes where I tried to help others run away and I was killed. Some of this I had seen during my past life regression with Kiana, and some of it was new.

During the session with Kiana, I was a bit unsure about what I was seeing because it could have just been my imagination, but this reader, Tiondra, didn't know me or Kiana. Everything she said gave me a deep, fulfilling feeling of confirmation. It felt like she was jogging my memories of who I was after a stroke. I felt so grateful that silent tears ran down my face. I was finding more pieces of my myself.

When we came to the segment where I could ask questions, I had so many that I wanted answered, but I knew we had a limited amount of time left in our one-hour session. I took a deep breath and asked for the purpose in my father's actions towards me in this lifetime. If we were going to run out of time, I absolutely needed to have that answer first.

Tiondra, shared with me that the man who was presently my birth father had been connected to me in a past life. In that lifetime, he was born with a great and powerful light, a light so strong that he would be able to bring smiles to others faces with a glance and heal them with a touch. But, when he was a child, that light was just a seed inside of him, waiting to bloom like an acorn unfolds into a mighty oak if it is cared for correctly.

Unfortunately, he was not nurtured. He was born into slavery and the plantation owner saw this light inside of him. The plantation owner couldn't define what he saw in the boy, but he knew it had to the be extinguished. He had the boy raped repeatedly and then forced him to rape others until there was no glimmer left in him, only confusion and pain.

I had been one of the victims the boy was forced to rape in that lifetime. He had also gotten me killed. All the suffering inside of him manifested in him hurting others. His soul had not healed or evolved past that point, so even now, he was carrying that same confusion and pain.

Wow, I was blown away. I couldn't hate him knowing all of this about him. There was a history to how he had gotten to this point. Though I still believed that he needed to be incarcerated so he wouldn't be able to harm anyone else, I could see myself really forgiving him now.

I still had a few minutes left and I didn't want to spend it on more questions about my father. I flipped to a new page in my journal where I was taking notes and wrote 'Contract' in big letters on the top before asking Tiondra, "What did I sign up to come to Earth for this time?"

"The soul you know as your father – you came for him. You signed up to teach him how to love again."

I couldn't say that I was surprised, but it was a bit frustrating. Here I was, in Costa Rica, teaching children, raising children, helping people to heal, seeing apparitions and doing tons of spiritual work with myself, and HE was my mission? I was doing all of this just to bring the benefits back to his undeserving ass? I mean, I had compassion for him, but he was still a pedophile. My purpose had to be bigger than teaching a pedophile how to love.

"Isn't there more to my life than that?" I asked Tiondra. "And how would I even go about teaching someone like him how to love? I can't even talk to him without him trying to manipulate me in some way."

"Yes," she replied. "You will do many great things and help many people, because you are a light. You can't help but to shine. But, you chose the family you did at the time that you did for a particular reason – for your father. After you resolve that mission, then your life purpose will expand to much larger work. You will be a leader in the ascension of the planet.

Okay, now this was sounding absurd. I can't say I didn't feel affirmation in my gut when she said the words, but how could I, a single mother who couldn't even lead my family out of messed up thought patterns, help lead the planet to ascension?

"And as far as teaching him how to love," she continued, "you've already been doing it. The genuine love that you've shared with him has been a great example for him. He may not recognize it now, but he will soon, and you will be a great part of his healing."

We had already exceeded the hour I booked, so I didn't ask anymore questions. I needed to process all of this anyway. After I hung up the phone, my mind wouldn't settle. I had heard twice now that I needed to heal my father, but I wasn't sure how to do that. One thing was for certain, if I was going to heal him, I needed to make a trip to Houston. Closing the 12 tabs I had open on my computer about 'spiritual answers', I began to search for flights. It was time to go home.

CHAPTER 12

I felt at ease knowing that I would be traveling back to Houston in two weeks. I didn't know how I would help my father, but I felt the method would come to me at the appropriate time. I wasn't worried about that, really, because I was so excited about just being open enough to be in the same room with him. I thought I'd never feel comfortable with that again. My openness showed me something beautiful about myself, that I was willing to forgive the unforgivable and love the unlovable. That was self-progress worth celebrating.

In the spirit of celebration, I arranged a babysitter for the children and called Kiana to set up a girls' night. It had been too long since I had been dancing! The thing about searching for answers is that each answer leads to another answer. It's like there are all these layers and when you think you're done, you're just beginning. But now, I was nearing the end of this particular journey. Whatever it took, I would heal my father. But first, I would dance until sunrise!

And dance we did. Kiana and I tore up the dance floor, saying yes to every man who asked us to Salsa and Bachata, and in between, dancing with each other. We sweated our festive sundresses all the way through by 4 a.m. and were quite ready to grab showers. Not wanting the night to end just yet, I suggested we bathe at the nearby beach.

We caught an uber there and stripped down under the moonlight to our undergarments, swimming into the ocean like children feeling the waves for the first time. We did backflips and headstands, held breath holding competitions, and laughed until our cheeks ached.

The best part of the night was when we swam over to a dilapidated wooden pier to sit on the edge. Right before we made it to the pier, we noticed a bright, blue glow in the water beneath it. Swimming closer, we saw hundreds of iridescent jellyfish. They appeared to be cerulean in one moment and turquoise the next. It was the most beautiful sight I'd witnessed in my life.

Not wanting to get stung by the gorgeous group, we turned back towards the shore, our arms and legs now tired from a long night of activity. The sun chose the perfect time to begin reddening the sky with a rosy glow.

When we made it back to our bags and got dressed, I noticed I had several missed calls from my mother. Why had she been calling me in the middle of the night? I returned her call immediately.

"Mama? You okay?" I greeted as soon as she answered.

"Yes, I'm fine. I have some bad news, though. I'm sorry to call you like this."

"You don't have to be sorry, Mama. What's going on?"

"I'm sorry. It's bad news…" her voice was cracking into heaving tears as she struggled to continue. "Your daddy dead. He died."

"What? How?" I collapsed into a seated position on the damp sand.

"He had a heart attack during a surgery for his cancer. I know all that bad happened between ya'll, but your daddy loved you. He did." Her voice was difficult to understand with the heavy breathing, like she was doing her best to fight back the tears.

"I know, Mama, I loved him too. I need some time, okay? Let me call you back later."

"Okay. I love you."

"I love you too, Mama."

CHAPTER 13

This had to be the worst news I'd gotten since I found out what my father had done. How could he just die? I was getting ready to come help. I had showered and taken the children to school, and then I came back home and climbed in the bed. I couldn't teach today. I needed some time.

"Mother?" I cried softly from under my thin blue blanket. I didn't know if she'd be able to hear me now or if she'd respond. Lately, it had been like she wasn't around.

"I'm here," I heard vibrate softly back to me. It was like she was in the air itself and the air was hugging me, comforting me, releasing the ache from my heart.

"It's too late," I whimpered, water pouring down my face. "I wanted to help him, but I wasn't fast enough. I've failed my contract. This is what I came for, and I failed."

"Is that what pains you, daughter? Truly?" she replied, the air embracing my shoulders now. I could only describe this feeling as mother's love. If I didn't believe she was my 'mother' before, I did now. I felt it.

"I never got to know him! I loved him without knowing what he was doing to me. It's like, what I believed our relationship was – it was all a lie. Then, I hated him for that. And now, I just found out that there was something beautiful inside him, authentically beautiful, that could be recovered..."

The tears wouldn't stop flowing as I continued purging my true feelings.

"...and I thought I would recover it. That would be my key to developing a genuine relationship with him. With that beauty, he would be deserving. And if he could be deserving, then I could too. I wouldn't be tainted anymore."

"You believe that he tainted you?" she asked.

"I mean, no relationship has ever worked out for me. Men hurt me or leave me. It must be that something is wrong with me – something I can't perceive that ties back to my father."

"Tell him that. Tell him all of that."

"Tell who?"

"Your birth father."

"I can't! He's gone now!"

"He's right here with you. He's in the room. Talk to him. Talk to his spirit."

I didn't take the blanket off my head because if I saw some ghost of my dad standing in my room, it would have been too much for me in that moment. However, I did as she instructed. I spoke to him.

"Why would you hurt me like that? I was just a baby, a toddler. You were supposed to protect me. Now, I'm broken. I fear for my son. How can I ever be a complete mother for him when I don't have a healthy relationship with men period, thanks to you?"

I stopped for a moment, and Mother urged me to go on.

"Yes, I forgive you. I forgave you. I wanted to come to Houston and help you heal, even. But, I need you to know that what you did is not okay. It did not make me stronger either. It made me weaker in ways I'm still discovering and healing from in my thirties."

"Tell him how he made you feel," Mother interjected.

"You made me hate you. You made me hate myself. You made me angry, sad, depressed, and empty. You made me feel worthless. You made me feel powerless. And why? All for your momentary pleasures. Was it worth it? I loved you so much, and you risked it all for perversions."

"Tell him what you want him to do," Mother said.

"I wanted you to heal. I want you to heal. I want you to relocate that light and beauty in yourself

109

that you had before you experienced all the pain and darkness. I want you to resurrect that light and be truly good."

"Ask him if he wants to do that," Mother directed.

"Do you want to heal? Do you want to be pure again? Do you want to be made new?"

I didn't hear an answer, but it seemed that the sunlight piercing through the fabric of my blanket shined twice as brightly.

"Tell him that if he wants to heal, he has to go to the light," Mother instructed.

"If you want to heal, go to the light. Go there and face yourself, so that you can be made new."

The light intensified and then I heard him. I heard his voice, not audibly like Mother's, but within my own mind.

"I will, baby. I will go to the light now. Thank you for believing in me. Thank you for loving me no matter what. I'm so sorry for what I did. I can't explain it, and I can't take it back, but I'm sorry. Goodbye."

I was so in shock that I couldn't respond for several minutes. When I collected myself, all I could say was, "Daddy?"

"He's gone," Mother replied. "You have guided your birth father back to the light."

"What? How? Was that some kind of ritual?"

"Yes, with your love. Thank you. Thank you so much. He deserves another chance to get it right."

"So, I completed my contract? Then, what do I do now?"

I removed the blanket from my head to see a multi-colored shimmer of light floating around the room. Some may say it was just a trick of the sunlight bouncing from the glass, but with all that was happening, I knew better.

She did not reply audibly again, but I felt the answer in my heart. It was time for me to simply be love and radiate that energy everywhere I went. To reconnect more deeply with my divine gifts. To spread the message in all my travels – "stop hurting yourselves, stop hurting each other, and stop hurting the earth." To lessen the suffering in the world through sharing healing light. To be at peace. To remain humble while identifying more and more with my higher self. To meet people where they are in their level of understanding. To speak truth. And, to always operate out of compassion.

Made in the USA
Columbia, SC
07 November 2024